for Zara

First published 2020 by Monmouth Press
Monmouth, Wales, UK

© Copyright Dion Dhorne, 2020

This book has been typeset in Optima.

ISBN-978-0992747497

Printed in the United Kingdom
by Biddles Books Ltd
Norfolk

10 9 8 7 6 5 4 3 2 1

Flora Flamingo

Dion Dhorne

Flora flamingo must learn how to fly.
She flaps and she flaps
but with try after try,
she just flails and she falls,
and she flops on the ground.

The longest of flutters
is only one bound.

'Oh pooey!' shouts Flora.
'I've tried hard all week.
And I'm fed up with failing!'
she says with a squeak.

'But you can! And
you will. You're a
bird!' says her dad.

'All flamingos can fly.
There's no need
to be sad.'

Her mum says, 'Our flock
must be going away,
for the summer has ended;
it's too cold to stay.

We need to fly off to a
warmer lagoon.
So get yourself ready –
we're leaving quite soon!'

'Watch this!' they both say, as they soar up on high,
and soon they are only two streaks in the sky.

But the rain
starts to pour:
Flora's feathers
are soggy.

She feels like
some seaweed
that's soaking
and boggy.

Then she hears
a small **PLOP**
with a very
small **SPLASH** and
a voice says,
'**HELLO!**'

And she spots the green flash
of a frog who says, 'Swim! It's amazing! It's cool.'
And, to show her, he leaps in and out of a pool.

With splashes,
he shows her the
frog way to swim.

Flora copies his
movements and
quickly jumps in!

But her legs get all tangled; they're wound up in knots.

And she bangs her poor head and sees stars, and then spots!

'Oh! How will I get to the African lakes?' Flora cries with a wail, as she shivers and shakes.

Then she jumps up in shock when she hears a loud **SNORT**!

And a horse neighs, 'Let's ride to the nearest large port!'

'You can sit on my back, and I'll canter so fast
that in no time you'll be in that boat with a mast.'

Flora climbs on
her back...

...and they trot all around. But she's jiggled and joggled with every small bound. And when the horse runs...

...she falls off with a thud - so happy to find herself
back in the mud!

'I am coming!'
she cries,
'Hold on now!
Wait for me!'

Then she floats
as she's running
- she's part of
the wind.

Oh! But
WHOOSH!

She is caught like a kite that is pinned,
and that flaps and that flaps as it tries to get free,
as the wind holds up Flora, who cries out,

WHEEEE-HEEEE!

The End